D0605659

Little, Brown and Company

Hachette Book Group
1290 Avenue of the Americas, New York, NY 10104
Visit us at lb-kids.com

LB kids is an imprint of Little, Brown and Company.
The LB kids name and logo are trademarks of Hachette Book Group, Inc.

The publisher is not responsible for websites (or their content) that are not owned by the publisher.

First Edition: April 2016

Library of Congress Control Number: 2015947165

ISBN 978-0-316-26074-9

10 9 8 7 6 5 4 3 2 1

IM

Printed in China

Welcome to the Mechazoic Era, a time when the Dinotrux roamed the land. Dinotrux are part dinosaur, part truck. They come in all shapes and sizes—big and small, wide and narrow, short and tall. The different Dinotrux always kept to themselves...they never worked together or helped one another out. That is, until an enthusiastic T-Trux changed everything.

One morning, there came a deep, low growl from inside a cave. Two eyes lit up the darkness like giant balls of fire. What was inside? Was it angry? Was it scary? Nope. It was Ty, a T-Trux, the mightiest of all the mighty Dinotrux and the very same T-Trux who would come to change everything for the Dinotrux. And he was just waking up after a good night's sleep.

Like he had every other morning, Ty had woken up hungry. He had a DINO-sized appetite! And what do Dinotrux like to eat? Ore, of course! Ty rolled up to a rock and lifted it up. Jackpot! There was some delicious ore waiting there for him. Ty took a big bite.

Suddenly, the ground rumbled as a nearby volcano erupted. This was no longer a morning like every other! Hot lava poured out of the volcano and toward the crater where Ty and some other Dinotrux lived. Ty knew they were in danger—it was time to flee!

Ty zoomed away as fast as he could, zigzagging to avoid hot falling rocks. He wondered how the other Dinotrux were doing. Would they all get away safely?

Just then, Ty rolled across a group of Ankylodumps trying to escape. One little Ankylodump was having trouble keeping up with his family. Ty knew what he had to do! He used his jaws to pick up the frightened Ankylodump and placed him safely on his father's bed.

Finally, Ty got far enough away that he was safe from the volcano. But he had no home anymore. He was tired and hungry after his escape. And he was injured—his broken tread trailed behind him. Ty wished he had a friend to help him. But Ty had no friends—Dinotrux did not get along with other Dinotrux. Ty felt sad and lonely.

The next morning, Ty went searching for a new home. He arrived at an enormous crater. He peeked over the edge and saw…

An amazing place! There were plants and trees, water and sunshine, and PLENTY of ore. Ty rushed inside. This wonderful place could be his new home!

Ty began to munch on some ore. While he ate, he noticed a small Reptool trying to push a big chunk of ore. The piece of ore was too big for him to lift. The Reptool looked very hungry. Ty knew what to do.

Ty gently used his wrecking-ball tail to break the big piece of ore into smaller pieces. Then he rolled one over to the little Reptool.

The hungry Reptool was surprised by Ty's help but grateful for the meal. He gobbled up the ore and then noticed Ty's broken tread. He knew he could fix it—Reptools can fix anything! But he was a little nervous to try. After all, this was a T-Trux, and they don't mix with Reptools. Could he trust the T-Trux? The Reptool decided to give the T-Trux a chance.

Grabbing a little bolt, the Reptool placed the tread back on its track and tightened the bolt with his tail. Ty's tread was as good as new.

"I am Revvit," the Reptool said.

"I am Ty Rux—but you can call me Ty! Thanks for fixing my tread!"

And just like that, Ty had a friend. Revvit hopped onto Ty's head, and Ty took Revvit for a spin. He couldn't wait to explore his new home!

Suddenly, another Dinotrux appeared. His name was D-Structs. He was a towering T-Trux, like Ty. But unlike Ty, he was not friendly. Not even a little bit friendly.

D-Structs was not happy to see Ty and Revvit. This was HIS crater. He didn't want anyone else to live in his crater or eat his ore. Ty thought D-Structs was acting like a bully—after all, there was plenty of ore to go around.

D-Structs did not like it when another Dinotrux tried to stand up to him. He knocked Ty down, then pinned him to the ground. "If you are still here when I get back, I will turn you into scrap," D-structs growled before he rolled away.

D-Structs was big and mean, but Ty wasn't going to back down to a bully. He had an idea: if he could get the other Dinotrux and Reptools in the crater to stand up to D-Structs with him, together they could defeat the bully.

“Let’s go recruit some others,” Ty told Revvit. But when he tried to talk to some Ankylodumps, they sped away. They thought he was a mean T-Trux and didn’t trust him.

But one Ankylodump *didn't* run away. His name was Ton-Ton. Ton-Ton was curious about the big T-Trux, so he listened to what Ty had to say. But Ton-Ton wasn't convinced... he wasn't sure he could trust Ty.

Ty and Revvit decided to move on and see if other Dinotrux wanted to join them. They met Skya, a tall Craneosaur. She laughed when she heard that Ty wanted the Dinotrux to team up against D-Structs. Dinotrux never worked together as a team!

Next, Ty tried to convince Dozer, a Dozeratops, to join him against D-Structs. Dozer thought having one T-Trux like D-Structs was bad enough. He didn't want another! He would make Ty leave the crater.

Dozer revved his engine and rushed toward Ty. He was going to shove Ty off the cliff! But Ty was too fast and moved out of the way. Dozer zoomed off the cliff, landed in a tar pit, and started to sink.

Ty couldn't just stand by—he had to help Dozer! He raced over to a rock wall and smashed off a big slab. Then, hoping to make a bridge to reach Dozer, he threw the slab into the tar pit. But it didn't work! The big slab started to sink.

Ton-Ton and Skya heard all the commotion and rushed over to see what was happening. They couldn't believe their eyes when they saw that a T-Trux was trying to help another Dinotrux. "We need a plan if we're going to save him!" Revvit yelled to Ty.

Ty and Revvit came up with a plan—they would BUILD a bridge! But they couldn't do it alone. Skya and Ton-Ton rolled over and offered to help.

And so, the Dinotrux finally worked together. Ty placed tree trunks in the tar pit and Skya pounded them into the ground. The bridge was coming together. But Dozer was sinking fast. Would they finish the bridge before Dozer disappeared into the tar?

When Dinotrux work together, they can do anything! In no time at all, they finished the bridge. As a team, they pulled Dozer out of the tar pit.

Ty was thrilled that Dozer was okay. And Dozer couldn't believe that Dinotrux—and a Reptool—had worked together to save him. Maybe teaming up against D-Structs wasn't such a bad idea after all....

Ty the T-Trux taught the other Dinotrux that they could work together and be friends. They agreed to be a team. They would stay in the crater together and stand up to the bully D-Structs...and whatever else came their way!

Ty was thrilled that Dozer was okay. And Dozer couldn't believe that Dinotrux—and a Reptool—had worked together to save him. Maybe teaming up against D-Structs wasn't such a bad idea after all....

Ty the T-Trux taught the other Dinotrux that they could work together and be friends. They agreed to be a team. They would stay in the crater together and stand up to the bully D-Structs...and whatever else came their way!